# Number 21

by Nancy Hundal

illustrated by Brian Deines

*Fitzhenry & Whiteside*

*With love to my sister Laurie and my brother Duncan,*
*who have kept on truckin' — and for the family who came later, Marty and Carole.*

*With special thanks to Barron and Ferguson's Jack and John*
— Nancy

Fitzhenry & Whiteside acknowledges with thanks
the Canada Council for the Arts, the Government of Canada
through the Book Publishing Industry Development Program (BPIDP),
and the Ontario Arts Council for their support of our publishing program.

Design by Wycliffe Smith.

Canadian Cataloguing in Publication Data

Hundal, Nancy, 1957-
Number 21

ISBN 1-55041-543-3

I. Deines, Brian.  II. Title.

PS8565.U5635N85 2001          jC813'.54          C00-932782-7
PZ7.H86Nu 2001

# Number 21

I am shouting and bouncing up and down. We are shouting and bouncing up and down, Laurie and Duncan and me.

Dad is so high up in the new truck, Number 21, and he also is bouncing up and down on the seat, gripping the wheel. He is smiling a big smile at us, pointing with one hand.

*Move out of the way!*
*Move out of the way!*

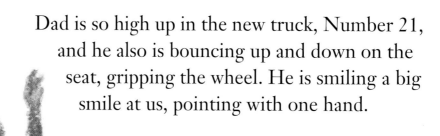

Dad's night truck, the one he drives home at night, has for so many years been Number 14. Now this new one, Number 21, will take its place.

Laurie, Duncan and me are standing on the steps leading from our backyard to the truck's parking space. We've been told many times to stay away from the night truck when it's being parked, but this time it's almost impossible to stay away.

Finally the engine sighs off. Inside the cab, Dad is checking and pulling on buttons and levers, like he always does.

He's taking so long! In spite of my impatience, my eyes are drawn to the letters and numbers over the dazzling red door.

All Dad's trucks are red, and this one, the twenty-first, has the name and number of our company on it like all the others.

J. Ferguson
261-1470

I slip forward to trace the parts of our phone number with my finger.

I know the delight of hearing a rumbling, roaring engine while standing on the street, and looking up quickly to see a blaze of red fly past with my telephone number on it. Sometimes it's even my dad, and he honks the horn, making everyone else in the street jump except me.

*Nancy, get back now. Your dad wants to open the...*

Door!

I'm a step back, the door is open, high up in the air, and he grins at us.

Mom is standing behind us, but can't move quickly enough to prevent all three of us from clambering onto the high sideboard.

Legs and arms flying, we all try to climb onto Dad's lap. He laughs at us, and slides over to let us in.

We are all interested in different parts of the truck. I head for the radio, because I love music. Then I pull on the wipers and squirt water at myself. Some funny cowboy music—Dad's favorite—snaps from the speaker when I twist the radio button.

Duncan checks out the steering wheel, yanking
it this way and that. He is crazy about driving
Dad's fleet of trucks.

Dad even lets him try the horn, but forgets to
warn Mom, who screams at the blast. She thinks
it's funny afterward.

Laurie likes the glove box, as she's always
curious about things. In it—after Dad unlocks it for
her—are a road map, flashlight, Dad's wallet and
sunglasses, and three chocolate bars.

Three chocolate bars! How did he
know she'd look in there?

We have to get out of the truck to
  eat. This new truck is very clean
  inside, not like Number 14.

Fourteen had greasy rags on
  the floor, and the seats were so
  dirty that we always put a towel
  down to protect our clothes.

Still, I think as I munch my
  chocolate, I liked that old truck.
  I'm going to miss it. Number 21 is
beautiful, but where is 14 parked
now? I feel a little sad.

Today is so hot. I'm sitting on the steps, and I can feel the sun pressing down on my forehead, my nose, my back. It is Sunday, so the pool at the park is closed. Even the sprinkler is broken—what luck.

My bathing suit is hanging limp on the clothesline. It looks hot too.

Just then Dad walks past me from the yard toward the truck. He is carrying the green garden hose.

At the same time, the clothesline begins to snake into the porch, carrying my suit with it. Dad comes back and turns on the tap. Where did the hose go? Where did my suit go?

*Nancy, come and put on your bathing suit.*
*Laurie and Duncan have theirs on already.*
*How come, Mom?*
*Because you're going to go swimming,*
*of course.*
*But where?*
*You'll see, honey. Come in now.*

I feel excited inside as I pull the straps of my suit over my arms. This seems like a mystery.

A new truck, a mystery, and a swim,
together on a hot day. I love that.

Mom leads us through the yard to the
steps. Nothing looks different, except for
the hose running past us and around the
back of the truck to the other side.

I follow it to the end, which is
hanging over the side of the
dump box, out of sight.
Suddenly, I understand.

Our wonderful truck is
now a wonderful pool!

With boosts, we all manage to get into
the box. The water is so cold—colder
than the day is hot. It gives my feet
a headache, but that doesn't matter.

We splash water over the sides, flop
face-first into the chill, dip our hair
forward into the water and then
slap it from side to side.

We have to scream a lot, to let out
the cold. It's not like a pool or the
ocean, where Mom says it's cold at first but
you get used to it.

You never get used to this.

Later, when the sun
starts to wobble
behind the garage, we
climb out, shivering.

Three towels are lying on
the grass, warm from the sun's
rub. We grab them.

Dad starts the truck, and
rumbles it out into the middle
of the lane. We watch as he
leans forward to pull the hoist,
and slowly the box begins to tilt.

Close to the cab, the box rises up
and up, while the end stays down.

A little water spills out at first, then
more than a little. Then suddenly
the gate pushes open, and a wild
waterfall crashes out, pouring
down the lane.

We can't even run across the grass
fast enough to see it hit the bottom
of the lane. It's that fast!

We are laughing and screaming and clapping.
This is almost better than the pool in the
back of the truck.

All the little rocks and sand that covered
the lane have washed down to the end.

Dad jumps out, the truck still running.
Mom is suddenly standing behind us,
looking at dad. He stares at the lane,
then looks at her.

His mouth is like an O.
Does he think that the water
taking out the lane is almost
better than a pool too?

Later, we watch Dad spread the new gravel down the lane. This is also fun.

Everything about Number 21 seems to be fun—for Laurie and Duncan and me.